Ellen Butler

In rhyme and measure

Poems

Ellen Butler

In rhyme and measure
Poems

ISBN/EAN: 9783337270223

Printed in Europe, USA, Canada, Australia, Japan

Cover: Foto ©Andreas Hilbeck / pixelio.de

More available books at **www.hansebooks.com**

IN RHYME AND MEASURE

IN RHYME AND MEASURE

POEMS

BY

ELLEN HAMLIN BUTLER

———————

CAMBRIDGE

JOHN WILSON AND SON

University Press

1892

TO

ANNA PAYNE BUTLER

AND

MRS. E. C. STEVENS.

CONTENTS.

8   *Contents.*

With borrowed thought, they say, we twist
Our verse, — not ours, — of lovers' tryst,
  Sunset and springtime, want and woe,
  Ring every change on "buds that blow,"
And "skies that melt in amethyst."

Each grinds, in turn, the selfsame grist, —
Yea, Shakespeare, Dante, search the list,
  And you may charge Boccaccio
  With borrowed thought.

What bard the critic dare resist?
Was Homer, too, a plagiarist?
  And Moses, — must we write him so?
  Then with uncovered head, for know
He pierced the brooding Spirit-mist
  With borrowed thought.

2

IN RHYME AND MEASURE.

THE TRINITY.

NATURE, herself a mystery,
Interprets best.   What would'st thou see?
Somewhere she has it pictured forth
Between the white fires of the north
And the dim arcs of midland bays,
Grand glimpses of God's grander ways.
Oh, sometimes on the cowering sense
Deep vistas break, so clear, intense,
We grasp the finite, life has set,
Whispering in awe, " Not yet, not yet! "
And learn, before the great unknown,
Love only bars us from the throne,
Yet bids immortal visions break
Upon the soul, for love's own sake.

From Gothic aisles, with cowled heads bent,
Perplexed, the sainted brethren went;
Leaving the dusk, where sacred thought
Had long in contemplation wrought,
Brooding in holy revery
Upon the mystic one in three;
When lo! a fair young boy, whose eyes
Revealed the angel in disguise,
Stopped them.

        "Behold," he cried, "the sun,
Resplendent, perfect! is he one
Or many?"

        "He is one," they said.
About the stately, shining head
A halo fell in shining rain.
Above the forest-girdled plain,
Prismatic splendors fold in fold
Lay trembling on the blue and gold,
The arch of promise.

        Tender, low,
The whispered voice came, "Will ye show
Another sun, or hath he blent
His rays with this frail element,
Disclosing all the secret soul

That ye may know the perfect whole?"
Oh, read the symbol, while ye can,
Of him who was the Son of Man.

One yearning gaze on the divine,
Transcendent beauty of the sign
They turned.   What eye unmoved shall see
The love and pain of Deity?
Sobbing the monks fell on their knees :
Night trembled through the chestnut trees ;
In cloister shadows hidden deep,
The great cathedral lay, asleep ;
But in the trance upon them cast,
They saw no future, felt no past.
When caught by a baptizing will
They rose, expectant, breathless, still.
Ah, neither sun nor shimmering bow
Shone in the rushing afterglow,
A matchless glory filled the sky,
And hark ! the angel, clear and high,
A star of flame, cried, " It is done !
Behold the Spirit, three or one ?"
Each turned him to his brother, then,
And stood transfigured ; not as men

They seemed, but in that awful light,
Archangels bearing back the night.

So stood they, till the gracious day
Had borne the miracle away ;
The solemn presence left the air
And wandering tapers called to prayer.
As one who looks on things unseen,
Each turned him to his old routine,
But on the threshold of his cell
Paused :

        Heard he but the vesper bell?
Or was it some far-falling strain
That came and went and came again,
The chant of an unnumbered host, —
" *Praise Father, Son, and Holy Ghost !* "

THE KING'S FOOL.

THE jester stood upon the lower stair,
  Before him passed the courtiers in a train ;
Proud faces, scented robes, and jewelled hair,
  Grave lips which smiled to hear his droll refrain.
And one bewildering beauty, looking down,
  Murmured, " How airily he scoffs all rule !
Sometimes I think I would disdain the crown,
  To be as happy as my monarch's fool."

A gray-haired statesman stopped to hear the word
  Of laughter tossed in light impertinence.
" What sway," he said, " denied to many a lord !
  The king, by him rebuked, knows no offence.
I sometimes wonder," and he paused again,
  " I, who by turns the master am, and tool,
If power would not come without the pain
  Had I but been the monarch's happy fool ! "

A cardinal in robes went slowly by,
  Viewing the motley garb, the cap and bells.
" Poor creature ! he is happier far than I,"
  He pondered.   " In that vacant bosom dwells
No thought but merriment ; no weightier mood
  Than moves yon ape, beside him on the stool.
Life for him lacks much that is great and good ;
  And yet I envy him, my monarch's fool."

The king called loudly, " Ho, we cannot dine
  Without the jester !   Look ye, noble sirs !
Here is a wight who knoweth good red wine,
  And careth not a whit for horse and spurs.
His head is empty.   He hath naught to hide.
  Life is for him no weary task or school.
Who is there of ye," and he faintly sighed,
  " Who would not live his monarch's happy fool ! "

Alone at midnight, underneath the moon,
  The jester stood, with motley doffed, and prayed :
" Lord, I am weary.   Send Thine angels soon
  To comfort me and give me strength," he said.

" My heart is sore with taunts and bitter sneers ;
  But, standing here amid the shadows cool,
I lift my soul, and none among the peers
  Can thrill with humble joy, as I, the fool."

3

REPOSE.

THE little moon from purple skies
　　Slips to a silver sea.
The dreaming world enchanted lies,
And peace like that of paradise
　　Steals gently over me.
Far out, beyond the phantom shore,
I drift with neither sail nor oar
To rock and dip, to fall and rise,
With idle hands and drooping eyes,
　　In happy reverie.

THE YACHTSMAN'S MESSAGE.

DEAREST, between whose quickened soul and mine,
   Great miles of summer swell,
I send thee love's most rare device and sign,
   A curling, twisted shell ;
Not from the shores where winds bring dreamy balms
And warm seas gleam 'twixt pillars of dark palms,
But where the breeze calls up, in fleeting calms,
   Welcome, and then farewell.

On the pine-girdled bowlders it had lain,
   Bleached white as sunless snow.
I took it from the cleft, in listless vein,
   Because I missed you so.
When suddenly a thought was born and swung
Into my languid pulses, met my tongue,
And on my cheek its vivid color flung,
   In ecstasy and pain.

I send this fretted shell, O thou true heart !
 It is not fair to see ;
But somewhat lies within and far apart,
 Which draws slow tears from me.
The little creature, in its blind life-quest,
Has vanished from the chambers of its nest,
As self died long ago within my breast,
 Died long ago for thee.

Then stole a mist, at daybreak, from the shore,
 Into its emptiness,
And ('t is my fancy) from the sunrise bore
 The seal of its caress ;
A hue of crimson stained with purple dye,
An amber glimmer from the brightening sky,
As love's soft morning came to me when I
 Dreamed life had ceased to bless.

Thou canst not see the glory wrapped within, —
 Trust me, it yet is there.
My love is silent, but there hath not been
 A deeper anywhere.
Trust me, for in our clear, set, stately ways,
The cold, sweet crystal of these modern days,

I cannot find one holy, burning phrase
    Of passion born, and prayer.

What lips have never learned, my heart shall tell,
    Deep in its rose-pearl throat.
Hold to thine ear this rough, wave-broken shell
    Where strange sea-voices float.
Feeling thy hand, their wandering tones shall wake
And my long yearning call arise and break
And blend them all, for thy beloved sake,
    In one heart-melting note !

CHOPIN.

Is it thy people's spirit in the strings,
    Or thine own soul, through suffering made pure?
    Some grief, some joy, beyond what we endure
Hath borne these strains.   Hark! how the cry begins
In broken songs that lift their beaten wings
    From doubt and longing, soaring, brave and sure,
    Until, in ecstasy and faith secure
They call, and out of heav'n an angel sings!
    Then sorrow wakes again the chant of woe;
My heart beats with the time and touch of pain, —
    The pain that wrung these quivering chords from thee.
So rang the harp of Orpheus, long ago,
    When looking back upon the dismal plain,
He saw the face of lost Eurydice.

AFTER "THE SEASON."

IT was August, I think, or July, when together
  We fled from the blaze of the heat to the shore.
'T was glorious, pulsing, voluptuous weather,
  The beaches were gayer than ever before,
With bathing and yachting and thronging of fashion
  (And hearts to be broken and hearts to be won),
With dancing and flirting and folly and passion :
  I was drawn to go back when the season was done.

It was twilight, — there never was twilight, remember,
  In the wild light of fierce electricity born, —
No witching waltz music stole out in November ;
  The sea broke in thunder, the wind blew his horn ;
That shore spread its curves like a new white creation,
  The sun-ravelled fog dropped from heaven, new spun ;
And only the cottages seemed desecration.
  I felt my soul stir when the season was done.

You know how it happened a week or two later :
  We sought in the mountains the best of hotels.
You have not forgotten that gem of a waiter,
  The jolly old Crœsus, those three pretty belles?
The buckboards and ponies, the grand wind-up party,
  The hasty good-by in the dim morning sun? —
A something so genial, so pleasant, so hearty,
  I was drawn to go back when the season was done.

I stood in the valley.   Up, up to the glory
  Rose cliff, dome, and peak to a crown set with snows,
Deep blue in the distance, here verdant, there hoary,
  Encircled forever by mighty repose.
The spires of the forest closed in all about me,
  I heard the new anthem of heaven begun,
Old memory hushed, and, my friend, can you doubt me? —
  God spoke to my soul when the season was done.

AVENGED.

In the old days, — whose scenes come from afar,
Like pictured poetry on an antique jar, —
A broken frieze, where slumbers holy art,
A sculptured god to touch a stoic's heart,
A quaint, carved jewel, in whose pulsing fire
Lives something of a passionate desire
We only dream of ; in those splendid days,
When life was sweet in every changing phase,
Because one knew not but at break of dawn,
Some nymph might steal across his woody lawn ;
Or, that before his wonder-smitten eye
A deity might sweep the trembling sky,
And fill his spirit with a great amaze
And rapture ; in those glorious old days,
A youth was given to Athens ; it is said
A flame had sparkled on his infant head.
So fair he was, the maidens turned again
And wept, because his beauty was a pain.

4

The wise men smiled and spake with weighty nod,
" There leaps the blood of a forgotten god ! "
His heart was noble with a lofty grace
Ennobling and chastening his face ;
And Athens knew no truer, dearer son
Than him my story calleth Procyon.
One morning, yet a little before day,
He left his restless couch, he could not say
Why, save within him, stirring visions burned,
A new desire and expectation yearned
And drove him forth.   In mingled fear and bliss
He sought the height of the Acropolis ;
And standing there in reverential awe,
All in the rosy, starlit dawn, he saw
The city at his feet ; a purple shade
Lay on the gleaming marble.   Half afraid
Of what he could not tell, he looked again.
Beyond the dim hues of that matchless plain
The soft, blue sea lay all unbroken, save
Where a fair fleet broke pearls from every wave,
Then dipped away to sink behind the sky
From proud Ægina, bound to Sicily.
Then turned he back upon a wondrous sight
That never more, as then, shall wake delight, —

The temples which once drew the gods to men,
And lo, the sunlight smote them ! Fearful, then,
He cast one glance upon the dazzling stone,
And crying, " Nay, I am not here alone !
What presence is this, terrible and sweet?"
Speechless, he fell beneath Athene's feet.
When once again, after a little space
Had passed, he woke, behold, a heavenly place —
A vast green vale cleft by a golden stream,
Whence rising like a dim, half-vanished dream,
A mountain peak gleamed from the purple cloud,
And when he saw that lightning-riven shroud
He knew Olympus. Springing upward, he
Waited, undaunted, for the god to be.
But straightway he was lifted from his feet,
And, borne by unseen wings 'mid odors sweet,
Was carried where immortals ever dwell.
It is not given tongue of man to tell
What there he saw, what ecstasy of bliss, —
An earthly muse may only dream of this, —
But when the rapturous twilight came at length,
Thrilling his veins with more than mortal strength,
Then cried the voice of him whom heroes fear,
" Choose what thou wilt, and Heaven is pleased to hear !

Favored of earthly ones, thou son of mine,
Ask of the gods, and every wish is thine."
Bewildered and astonished, it was long
Ere Procyon spake ; then, beautiful and strong,
He knelt before the great and mighty one.
"O Zeus ! what ever have I said or done
To win thy favor?　Yet, since it is given
I ask these gifts of bounteous smiling Heaven :
Be thou, first, my protector, that I may
Live like a god until that dreary day
When I must go into the world of shades.
And, that I reach the fair Elysian glades,
Let Pluto frown not on my death alarms
But lay me in Proserpine's white arms.
Great Hera, awful goddess ! by my side
Deign to become my patroness and guide !
Fierce Ares, stoop my arms in war to bless !
Sweet Aphrodite, in thy tenderness
Favor my suit in love ! and with me go,
Blind Eros, with thy strong heart-seeking bow !
May fair Apollo guard me in the race,
And Artemis pour blessings on the chase,
And, that I skilled in lore and wisdom be,
Athene, listen and be kind to me !

I would prevail as Heaven in all things. This
I ask ; I therefore cannot ask amiss."
"Go forth," said Zeus ; "thy prayer is heard ; alone
Of the world's best, we claim thee for our own."
Then Procyon turned ; and, lo, before him stood
Poseidon in his vesture wild and rude.
"Go, son of gods, go back to earth," cried he,
"And ponder if thou hast no need of me !"
He vanished ; and behold, with limping tread
And flames of fire about his tawny head,
Hephaistos came. In wrathful tone called he,
"Go back! Heed well, thou askest naught of me !"
He fled with scorching breath ; and, sore afraid,
The youth went on to meet a pure-eyed maid,
Hestia, the beautiful and chaste. "Yea, flee,"
She said ; "thou hast no gifts to ask of me !"
Behind her, scattering plenty from her horn,
Demeter stood, majestic 'mid the corn.
"Go on," she said in sorrow ; "thou shalt see,
Some day, what gifts I had in store for thee."
Outside the portal, in a shadowy place
Stood Hermes, graceful, airy, on his face
A mocking smile. His wingèd rod he flung
Aloft, and cried in silver, sneering tongue,

"Go back to earth! See what its joys may be!
Here is a man who hath no need of me!"

Years passed. I know not, but those far years seem
To float into the centuries like a dream.
To manhood Procyon came, — a mighty man,
Who gathered mighty things in one brief span
Of eighty years. Immovable, serene,
He lived apart. Upon that awful mien
No weakness dwelt. Success was his, indeed.
Alas, success! His every word and deed
Potent but always terrible. He knew
Himself alone ; and to that self he drew
All things of worth to feed his will and pride,
Then cast them in cold cruelty aside.
Dreadful in war, relentless in the chase,
In love triumphant, ruthless, without grace,
He never saw the fury by his fate
Ever pursuing him until too late,
When on his couch he felt his end so near
He scarce could look upon the sunset clear
Outside his open door. Then all the past
Rose up accusing ; and he cried at last :
"Do I, the prince of men, come thus to stand

Upon the borders of an unknown land?
Must I alone, uncomforted, go down
To the black river? Bring my laurel crown
And spear and shield! They cannot aid me more!
Is there no love? Who stands outside my door?"
And, lo, between him and the amber skies
Stood Hermes, with his glorious, mocking eyes!
" Dost thou lie *here*, favored of Heaven's best,
Procyon?" he said. "Art thou about to rest
The head that Hera loved once to caress
Under the sod? Thus do the great gods bless,
Only to slay! What dost thou leave behind?
No goodly handiwork to cheer mankind,
No noble trophy of Hephaistos' art
To ease the burdens of the laboring heart;
Thou hast despised him. Earth did never bear
One harvest for thy sickle's gleam to share;
Demeter thou didst scorn. Likewise the sea,
Poseidon's treasure-house, hath yielded thee
No tribute. Neither wife nor child were thine;
Thy household fires were never Hestia's shrine.
Thou hadst none that might wear her holy name;
Love was to thee dishonor and a shame.
Thou leavest nothing to thy fellow-men, —

Not one poor word ! Dost thou remember when
I met thee at the portal, — I, who reach
The heart of Zeus with all-prevailing speech ?
My power had wreathed thy name for endless time,
My gifts had made thy memory sublime ;
But since no generous heart was found in thee,
Thou art forgotten to posterity.
' Favored of Heaven ! ' I said ; yea, get thee hence !
The world hath seen thee brought to impotence ;
On thine old age shall life its hunger wreak ! ''
Then Procyon raised his head and strove to speak,
Whispering, " Hermes, think that I was young.
Grant me thy grace, thou of the silver tongue ;
Let me but speak *one word* that may redeem
My memory from utter death ! '' A gleam
Stole o'er the icy features of the god.
He lifted high his twisted, wingéd rod,
And — solemn miracle ! All Athens heard
A voice that thundered till the deep earth stirred,
That rent the white stone, sundered e'en the clods,
Crying, " Beware the vengeance of the gods ! ''
And men, with blanching faces, looked upon
Each other, saying, " Then spake Procyon.''
Fearful, yet pitying, at break of day

Kind eyes looked down upon his perfect clay,
Murmuring, " He seemeth gentler than of yore.
Perchance in sleep he found the blessed shore."

Thou, whose bright spirit wings are now unfurled,
If thou wouldst shine in heaven, bless thy world ;
And if thou wouldst escape the scorpion rods,
Beware the vengeance of the slighted gods.

5

A "NORTHERN MORNING."

Out of the night
A silver bar
Of light
Streams up to the cold North Star !
A single flame that has come and gone,
But the sky is filled with a dream of dawn ;
A glimmer of rose without its glow !
The sudden flash of a fairy fire !
And luminous billows break and flow,
Surging and swelling to and fro,
Ever ascending, broader, higher,
Flashing, flying, vanishing, dying,
Throbbing with soulless and passionless power,
Writhing, darting, scattering, parting,
Drowning the stars in the icy shower !

Behold a line of glittering spears
Out of the nebulous mass appears ;

And giant armies advance at will,
Phantom battalions, spectral, still.
See how they whirl and bend and toss
Their helmets of steel and plumes of snow!
They rise and mingle and dance and cross
To melt in the strange, weird light below ;
Then white, cold flames to the zenith dart,
As if life, from being awhile apart,
Went shimmering, shifting, up the sky
In wild, delirious ecstasy ;
And, fleeing madly, they quiver and flare —
Behold, there is nought but empty air !
But out of the silent heavens, far,
Again a single silvery bar,
        Serenely white,
        Streams up the night,
And fades away 'neath the cold North Star.

LOVE'S TRIUMPH.

PAIN stirred his wild, fierce fires afresh,
   And precious things he cast therein.
The awful flame that sunders flesh,
   From spirit and the soul from sin,
Leaped up to smite the furnace wall;
   And lo, a little space apart,
Three angels watched the embers fall
   And flame upon a broken heart.

All in the seething light it lay,
   Burned inward to its very core;
But Patience would not turn away,
   Nor heed the martyrdom she bore.
Pale, motionless, and weary-eyed,
   She marked Pain's awful ministry,
Nor plead one pang be turned aside,
   Nor spared one mortal agony.

Faith stood beside her, unaware
  That crimson lights crept round her feet :
I saw a halo on her hair ;
  I saw her eyes, transcendent, sweet.
And in the shadow Hope delayed,
  With lips that smiled away her fears :
And yet the lurid glory made
  Soft rainbows in unfallen tears.

Hearken ! the sweep of mighty wings !
  Love comes, unbidden and alone.
Into the furnace depths he springs
  And stoops as one who finds his own ;
He stands upon the neck of Pain,
  And, resting like a tender dove,
A snow-white heart on his is lain,
  The treasure of immortal Love !

SISTERS.

I.

As modest as her dainty dress,
Unconscious as the light about her,
   She wins your judgment to confess
      Our world were poor without her.
With dignity and grace self-taught,
She lives her home life, all unheeding
   That others see in word and thought
      Her noble, gentle breeding, —
A manner culture cannot mend,
A way that makes us more than love her;
   She will not learn to condescend,
      The critic is above her.
A sympathy that wakes a smile
Is hers, with this magnetic mission, —
   You know she has your own the while
      By subtile intuition.

Sensitive, trusting, fearful lest
Her step may crush a wayside flower,
   Eager to give and do her best
      To beautify the hour,
She never dreams her loving own
Are not the only ones who greet her
   With reverence in look and tone,
      Believing life is sweeter
Because her brown eyes saw the day, —
Because she comes to us and lingers,
   Smoothing the troubles from our way
      With dear, caressing fingers.

II.

TALL, fair, and proud, did ever fear
Or doubt one moment cloud her vision?
   Her profile, well-defined and clear,
      Shows quiet, calm decision.
She meets the world without a boast,
To challenge it on equal basis,
   And takes its offers with the most
      Impassible of faces.
Strong in the armor of her youth,

She sets its evils at defiance,
  And should it compromise the truth,
    Would scorn to make alliance.
But yet how tender is the heart
Beneath a panoply so royal !
  How brave to suffer wound or smart,
    Unwavering and loyal !
She cuts the Gordian knots we bring
To her, with clear and quick discerning;
  She finds some good in everything
    Around her to be learning.
Her logic knows a brighter way
Than all our older wisdom teaches,
  And still it seems but yesterday
    We conned her baby speeches !
If from her every maiden mood
Sweet promises our love may borrow,
  We bless the gracious womanhood
    That blooms for us to-morrow.

A SEA OF GRASSES.

It lay in an upland vale. Around it
The purple pines of the hillside bound it, —
The world, I fancy, had never found it,
  Lying close to the sky.
Never a breaker called desolation,
Only a whispering palpitation
Broke on the midsummer meditation,
  When the south wind came by.

There were deep, green hues in its feathery billows,
And golden nests for the light's soft pillows,
There were rich, dark shadows under the willows
  Near to its hither side.
No plummet sounded its tremulous mazes,
Crowned with the foam of the tilting daisies,
It shifted, unruffled, its faery phases
  In mimic play of the tide.

Stirred by some tricksy and breeze-born notion,
It caught the whirl of a vanished motion,
Or rose and fell like the far-off ocean
    Singing on distant bars.
No shallop sign on its surface drifted,
Save a phantom sail when the storm-mist lifted,
And a wake where the elf fleet left it rifted,
    Sailing under the stars.

But oh, to-day in the clear, cool gleaming,
Low voices stole on my last, faint dreaming,
A ring and a flash on my senses streaming,
    A rhythm that grew with dawn.
The noon air, fierce with its heat and thunder,
By scents of Eden is parted asunder.
But the fireflies and the moon will wonder,
    For the summer sea is gone.

LONELINESS.

I.

I DRAW the curtain back, my eyes still wet
With homesick tears. Against a clear west set,
The strange, weird landscape mocks my yearning mood ;
A long scarred hill, a rocky wall, a wood,
A road half lost amid the fern and brake,
A moonlit breadth of silent stretching lake.
And memory calls back the yesternight ;
Soft color, music, tumult, and delight ;
Glad faces all around me. Everywhere
A city's splendor, flaming up the air.
And grief sobs wildly in its first excess,
" How can I bear my utter loneliness ! "

II.

I draw the curtain back, as one who knows
And fears to look. Wrapped in a great repose,
The long hill in the sunset looks farewell,
O little year ! How could my faint heart tell

What waited me?   Dear Love, wilt thou not call
My name once more beside yon rugged wall?
Among the city's jargons, will no tone
Come from the forest mingled with their own?
How shall my life apart from thee be spent,
And this beloved scene grown eloquent
With thee?   Look down, bend out of heaven to bless,
And pray God for me in my loneliness.

III.

I draw the curtain back.   There is no change.
Perchance a softer curve sweeps up the range.
Years leave their mantle on the bald old scars,
These years.   I lean against the window bars,
And watch the dark lake shimmering in the breeze,
The wall, the wood, that grave behind the trees.
Time hath not left my soul one bitter sting,
Life learned its mission through its suffering.
Once more I stand, expectant and apart,
Immortal voices singing in my heart,
And feel, as earth's companionships grow less,
The benediction of my loneliness.

FEBRUARY, 1886.

THE VOICE OF MAINE.

[Written for the Reunion of the Maine Legislature, January, 1886.]

GREECE, in her day of power, saw
   Amid her matchless forms of stone,
A race, by nature's happiest law,
   More perfect. On her sea-swept throne
She mourned the grace of which they died,
   And wept for sterner clay again.
Be mine the nobler Spartan pride;
   Behold my sons, the sons of Maine!

Rome strewed the streets with garlands when
   Her legions came with captive bands.
Those were the days of mighty men;
   But those, the days of wasted lands;
Behold my warriors come! No sound
   Of wailing breaks the martial strain,
No blood of slaves is on the crowned.
   These are my sons, the sons of Maine!

These are my sons ! No mystic sage
    Hath reverence like those who read
The prophecy on war's dark page,
    And bade the land be comforted.
For some with counsel, some with sword,
    Went down, an awful cup to drain,
And knew the fiat of the Lord.
    These are my sons, the sons of Maine !

The nation knows my children, they
    Who carry in their souls and wills
Some mood that must command and sway
    A birthright of their frost-hewn hills.
And those who knew no vaunted part,
    Still toiled in silence for my gain,
All share the bounties of my heart.
    These are my sons, the sons of Maine !

Young hearts are here, who only wear
    The earlier glory manhood yields.
They hold my future ; wait to bear
    Fresh harvests from far broader fields.
To-day there is no thought of strife,
    No ghost of old, forgotten pain.

Brethren, whose life is all my life,
   These are my sons, the sons of Maine!

O voices, winter-clear, awake
   In all the wild familiar shrines;
In thunder on the great shores break,
   Call from the deathless mountain pines.
The chant that lulled their cradle rest
   Is sweet to homesick heart and brain;
Cry "Welcome!" down each cliff and crest
   For these, my sons, the sons of Maine!

HAPPINESS.

To throb with tides of perfect health
    In glad, free veins;
To pulse with life that knows no pains,
    Whose restless wealth
Of energy, desire, and will
Increase and give, increasing still,
To meet a sphere which power shall fill,
    Nor ills destroy;
While thought and act together thrill, —
    Oh, this is joy!

To move with conscious scope, and grasp
    Truth's end and plan;
To leap beyond that bond of man,
    Time's iron clasp;
To bend an intellect so keen
It knows no fault, on the unseen,

And mark what shall be and hath been
    Immortally;
Forever learning, — this must mean
    Mind's victory!

To feel all hopes, all ends, all aims
    Blending to one,
Then waken to a life begun
    With double claims;
Yielding to glorious hopes which roll
Upon the wondering heart and soul;
Rising beyond doubt's sad control
    To where, above
Sweet youth, life waits its finished whole, —
    Ah, that is love!

To fold this mortal vesture by;
    To see at last
The gray earth slip into the past,
    And heaven draw nigh;
Waiting with nothing more to fret
The spirit learning to forget
Old memories, that sin has set
    Till life shall cease;

7

To rest where death and trust have met, —
  Oh, that is peace!

To watch, in overwhelming awe,
    Faith's shadow lift;
To gaze while those vast glories shift
    That Moses saw;
To meet the terrible White Throne;
To hear One star-creating Tone
Call this poor, trembling soul His own,
    Eternally, —
Oh, this, my heart, and this alone,
    Is ecstasy.

THE RETREAT OF THE FOG.

OVER the harbor, sullen and still,
A gray fog stretches its mantle chill,
Wrapping its folds round cove and hill,
   With cold and shadowy hands.
The idle vessels rock to and fro,
Or rise and dip in a rhythm slow
On the silent tide, that is ebbing low
   Over the dreary sands.

A flush of rose from the upper air
Suffuses the mist, and everywhere
A glow and a radiance, wondrous fair,
   Quiver upon the deep ;
For overhead, like a living thing,
A breeze from the west comes wandering,
The breath of the sunshine on his wing,
   Waking the world from sleep.

He breathes on the shifting, trembling mist,
And, lo, it severs!   The waves are kissed
With mingled fire and amethyst,
    Leaping to life anew.
Through golden vapors that eastward stream
The far-off heavens appear, and gleam
Like visions of Paradise in a dream,
    Tenderly soft and blue.

Deep in the purpling evening light
Island on island floats in sight —
Out of a veil of billowy white,
    Shimmering down the bay.
Far away, on the ocean's brim,
Sail the ships in the distance dim,
Over the pale horizon's rim,
    Into the dying day.

Night has fallen, serene and clear,
The strange, mysterious stars appear,
And out of my soul a voice of cheer
    Speaks silently to me ;
A blessed peace on my heart is shed,
My weary spirit is comforted,
For doubt and despair together fled
    When the fog went out to sea.

TWO PICTURES OF CHILDHOOD.

[A. D. 400.]

HE stops to watch the fountain twisting high its silver
thread ;
And whosoever runs may read in figure, movement,
eye,
The glory and the beauty from patrician sources fed,
Yet all his eager, childish fire quenched by satiety.
Those languid limbs have never known the waking
touch of pain ;
Indifferent, he sees the world go by his marble home';
Scoffs at the gods with baby lips too early taught
disdain,
Dreaming there is no higher lot than his — a son
of Rome.

He stands beside the Baltic Sea, a boy with tawny hair,
Straining his eyes to see, beyond the mingled sleet
and spray,

Two mighty birds at battle in the dusky middle air,
  Exulting in their struggle, and half-envious of their
    prey.
Mercy hath never found a place in his relentless mind ;
  He seeks within the Northern Lights the visions of
    his creed,
Knowing the Valkyr maidens to the warrior dead are
    kind,
  And feeling in his heart the will to satisfy his need.

O little child, born to the splendor of this latter age,
  Whose fairy tale is science and whose alphabet is
    truth,
Know this, — that God hath given thee the centuries'
    heritage,
  From Roman and Barbarian to draw thy matchless
    youth.
A thousand strange, opposing moods thy heart and
    purpose thrill ;
  A thousand contradictions rise and vanish in thy
    face ;
God blendeth all in thee, a new, exalted sphere to fill,
  And crowned them with the gifts of Knowledge,
    Love,· and Christian Grace.

BOUND SEAWARD.

THE river shores drop lower, and wreathe
    A fringe of rock-beaten snow;
O'er miles of glory the wild airs breathe,
    And sea-born mysteries blow.
The waters sink in a grander roll,
    And rise in a lighter spray;
We are speeding down, O my happy soul,
    Speeding down to the bay!

The wavering coast tipped with a light
    Goes out. The horizon sweeps
Round and round in a wonderful night
    Where nothing awakes or sleeps.
But exquisite life, that hath no part
    With the continent left to lee,
Beats with the ocean into my heart,
    That is winging away to sea.

The bonds of being retreat. We feel
   The wind from a broader sky,
A rush of billows under the keel,
   That quivers with prophecy.
Up to the morn we toss the sail,
   Our pilot knows not delay,
But catches· favor from every gale.
   We are speeding down to the bay!

The land will darken, will fade, will end,
   With faith for a beacon star,
And sweet, still night on our bark ascend
   Across the last vanishing bar.
But with the Spirit below, above,
   Breathing the life to be,
What matter when those currents of love
   Bear us away to sea!

STEAMER " PENOBSCOT,"
   Sept. 21, 1885. ·

THREE SONGS.

"I WILL sing a song to the world," he said,
  "The world, that a rhyme will please;"
And musical words from his light lips sped,
  With careless, half-scornful ease.
But never an eye the brighter shone,
  And never a smile or sigh
Came up to the poet, who sang alone;
  For the world went hurrying by.

"I will sing a song to the cultured few!"
  He cried with a covert sneer;
And brilliant fancies in phrases new
  He fashioned, for many a year.
He sent them forth while he stood aloof,
  And waited in calm disdain;
But the critic spoiled their shining woof,
  And sent them to him again.

8

"I will sing a song to my dying love!"
  He whispered in agony;
" Perchance at the birth of the life above,
  She will hearken and pity me!"
But she drifted back from the arms of death,
  At his summons so wild and sweet;
And lo! the world, with a sob in its breath,
  Lay down at the poet's feet.

WHEN SPRING COMES UP THE KENNEBEC.

GAUNT, iron reefs crouch low and grim,
   Like dragons waiting for their prey,
Heard through the wild March twilight dim,
   In threatening roar of surf and spray.
Beyond their jagged foreheads lie
Drear waves, drear shores, and drearier sky,
   Moaning above some tragic spot,
Whose eddies kiss a sunken wreck.
   Ah me, it is a woful lot
Of them who seek and enter not
   The gateways of the Kennebec !

Dread, mystic portals ! who shall tell
   Why God hath bid those warders stand
Guarding so ruthlessly and well
   The borders of a charmèd land.
About them, haunting voices wail,
   But see ! a single roseate sail

Trembles upon the mist, and lo,
  The sun breaks forth, and it is gone !
Yet the uprushing waters know
  The magic bark is flitting on,
Forever followed by the glow
  Of life and joy in double dawn.
Stark marsh-lands waken out of death,
  To feel their own gray wretchedness,
Again, the pines with richer breath
  Challenge old Winter, pitiless.
And far up o'er the ice-leagues, thrills
  A message to the mute, sad hills.

"Oh, waken, waken, everywhere !
  The fairy argosy of Spring
Flashes by icy-caped Seguin.
  Her foremost shallop rocks, to-day,
Light-winged, on Merrymeeting Bay.
  Hark to the laughter in the air
Where happy songs in carols break
And life comes murmuring in the wake !
  From every spar the sunbeams fall,
Sweet treasure loads the gleaming deck,
  Oh, waken, waken, waken all !
For Spring comes up the Kennebec !"

They hear, the great ice-leagues, they hear,
  And call to every hill, "Oh, see
What gems the river sweeps, how near
  Is the delivering argosy?"
"So far we may not see it yet,
  But courage! In the south is set
A banner like a golden flame.
  Arise! for Winter yields, and greet
  The couriers; go forth to meet
Who come in this the conqueror's name."

Adown the stream, whose waters blue
  Leap to the misty sun, anew,
Winter's great squadrons, captive, go
  To the deliverer's fleet, below.
What eye hath seen him yield his hosts?
What ear hath heard the victor's cry?
But, frailer than the morning ghosts,
  They melt beneath the tender sky.
Bleak, watching hills, ye wait not long,
  A band of color stains the tide,
From willows quivering with song,
  The deepening tints soar out and glide
Across the happy fields, and far
  Up naked cliff and cruel scar;

Broadening in clearer, fuller hue;
　　Until the forest kings look forth
And shout in mighty triumph to
　　The Lake of the Enchanted North.
Pulsing with hope, the sweet notes reach
　　Its waters, and soft breezes blow
Across the silent, curving beach,
　　The balm of woods without their snow.
" Oh, waken, waken everywhere ! "
The hushed earth wraps herself in prayer.
From sparkling lakes and heaven-crowned heights,
　　Long valleys wreathed in new delights ;
　　　　From winding lengths of river, goes
　　　　The benediction of repose.
And where the floods lie, wide and deep,
　　The reefs a dreaming vigil keep ;
　　Upon the farthest outward isle,
On crag and cove and wave-worn neck,
　　Beauty leaps forth to meet God's smile,
For Spring comes up the Kennebec !

THE DAY AFTER.

MILLY is dead! Don't tell me so!
  Of Farmer Harrison's girls the last
That was left at home, and the first to go!
  Yesterday — yesterday — over and past.
I never hear what is happening, though,
  Living so far and out of the way,
And this is awful and sudden — oh,
  I can't believe what you say!

Yesterday — why, I sat and saw
  The old snow melt on the cellar door;
I heard a crow in the gray pine caw;
  It seemed like the spring ten years before,
When she and Mary and Josephine
  Came with their father, — the little one
Sitting so smiling in between,
  With her hair all bright in the sun.

Josephine, "she was the smartest." Yes,
    They said she studied, a long, long while,
Latin and French and Astronomy
    And ever so much. Then what makes me smile?
Well, I was thinking that Milly speaks
    Something better than French, and knows
Why the stars shine so, why that sunset streak
    Is just the color of rose.

Mary — I s'pose she has n't heard yet,
    Travelling round with her Uncle John.
She was the beauty, and won't forget
    To choose the mourning that she puts on.
No, I would n't be hard on her ;
    But there she is, in that heathen Rome,
And Josephine making a name and stir,
    While Milly lies dead at home.

" Somebody had to stay and do?
    She was a home girl?" Bless her then.
How kind and happy and sweet and true
    She was ! What a woman she might have been !
Ah, she was a child of these high blue hills ;
    And, just as the flowers and ferns are given,

To be taken away when the first frost chills,
    She was taken away — to heaven.

Gentle and Christlike and well content
    And patient, — perhaps where she is to-night,
These things count more than a lifetime spent
    In learning. I'd rather my *heart* was right.
And for beauty! — oh, to be white and good!
    Of a thousand thousand created things,
What is like that soul in its maidenhood,
    When yesterday gave it wings?

9

COMFORTED.

I 'D just been desperate all that day; I could n't stand
    one thing more.
The work was piling and piling up, like an awful
    mountain before.
I gave my dish-cloth a twist and wring, — the wring
    of my bitterest mood, —
And said, " If the Lord *is* tender, or cares, he 'll show
    me a token for good."

And Milly turned, as she stood outside, in her pretty,
    new figured gown ;
I saw the tears in her big blue eyes. God bless her !
    They seemed·to drown
A little of all I was suffering. She waited, and then
    said she,
" Perhaps He sends us some tokens that we do not
    look to see."

When she was gone, I sat down and cried, with my
    head on the old red shawl;
I almost thought there was n't a God to plan for this
    world at all!
But after I 'd cried my tears away, I thought of what
    Milly had said, —
I thought of it all the afternoon, and when I had gone
    to bed.   .

In the morning I went to the door; and there was my
    cactus at last in bloom, —
A great, red, glorious blossom, that had burst 'twixt
    the light and the gloom.
And when I looked deep into its heart, I felt a kind
    of an awe;
That sheaf of stamens! that perfect cup! but that
    was n't all I saw.

I gazed at the gnarly, prickly plant, so bare and
    crooked and dry,
With that blossom just like a rosy star dropped out of
    the morning sky,
Then sank to my knees beside the door; and there,
    on the cold, wet sod,
I knew there was One who cared for me, and He was
    the loving God.

For, oh, if He has the power to make such a flower,
    by love divine,
Perhaps He will bring a pure, white soul from such
    a poor life as mine.
It is dry and twisted and dreary, filled up with my
    household dust;
But, ah, I have seen His token, and I know I can wait
    and trust.

Somehow the day became solemn; and long ere the
    sun was low,
I took the Bible and read the words I had treasured
    so long ago.
The stars, they whispered immortal things of a Great
    Heart over me;
And I prayed, as I pray with every night, "Lord,
    open my eyes to see."

FAITHFUL.

Yes, it was Sunday afternoon, the day before the
　"Fourth,"
And William's folks were coming down to see us from
　the North;
The sky was blinding hot, the fields quivering and
　dazzling lay,
Along the roadside to the hills, just ready for the hay.

I did n't feel like company, and Jacob could n't plan
To take me to the Valley church, — he does it when he
　can, —
And so I took the Bible down to read some cheering text,
But, there, the first words left me more discouraged and
　perplexed.

" He that is faithful (seemed like she) in that which is
　least " — oh,
I thought how I had worked that week, and some things
　had to go;

All those long blazing summer days, from very peep of
    dawn,
I'd left so many tasks half-done, to start some other on.

I could n't make the time, and ah, it sickened me to
    find
How many duties waited me, what new ones pressed
    behind.
And then that Scripture — how it burned into my heart
    so sore !
Just then a shadow, cool and still, fell on me from the
    door.

And there was Milly, smiling, as a star smiles in the
    west.
She came and knelt beside my chair; then, somehow,
    I *felt* rest.
She brought the church right home to me, a blessing
    seemed to fall,
And with the Bible in my lap, I sat and told her all.

She laughed, — but it was pitiful, — and laid her sweet
    young face
Against my cheeks, soft whispering, " It is not works,
    but grace ;

God knows you have not time enough ; He sees the
busy care,
But when you add the worry on, you take a double
share.

"When Martha told Him all her toils, He did not make
them less,
But said she needed one thing more, to sanctify and
bless ;
The perfect work may not be whole, He knows how
hard we strain ;
He will accept unfinished deeds, and spare reproachful
pain.

" The best we have, the best we give " —her voice was
broken, low —
" Are blessed only in His sight as love can make them
so ;
He asks not what we cannot do; His pity meets our
needs,
And takes, instead, submissive trust, and cheerful,
patient deeds.

"'Faithful'?— it is no stern, hard word, for us to
    dread to speak.
What can it mean but *full of faith ?*— not judgment
    for the weak !"
I caught the Bible to my heart; I'd never hoped to find
Such comfort in that little verse I'd twisted in my
    mind.

The bad days come; I do my best, yet something has
    to lie
Half-finished with the setting sun, however hard I try;
But now I cast my care on Him, that I may "faithful
    be,"
And I believe the Lord Himself does up that work
    for me.

BLUE SKIES.

Sᴀᴅ twilight trails her heavy clouds
   Into the night. One sullen zone
Of mist, in nearer circling shrouds,
   Sweeps out the hills our love has known.
Cold hours go sobbing overhead,
   When hark ! the west wind's herald cries ;
And by his sweet persuasion led,
Behold one far, faint sparkle sped
   Through rifted vapors. Sleep, glad eyes,
Dream happy things. Above are spread
      Blue skies !

Life, eager heart of mine, is storm,
   Thou canst not part the lowering years.
Closer and deeper, phantoms form,
   Thy near horizon veils in tears, —
The world drifts from thy yearning sight ;

But hark ! what free wind hither flies,
Singing of strange, unseen delight?
A star shines in the death-wrack's flight !
Dream thou of morn and Paradise,
Over thy grave shall watch, to-night,
Blue skies !

November, 1885.

A SONG OF THE END.

WHEN life had done with her youth, no more
　　To struggle ; when life had wept
And laughed at her weeping ; when her store
Of treasures broke on the tomb's cold floor,
　　She laid her down and slept.

But she woke at the hour when all else sleeps
　　And eternity draws nigh ;
With eyes like thine own, where patience keeps
Watch o'er the heart's unsounded deeps,
　　She looked on the cold, black sky.

" I have wakened to go to my graves," she said,
　　" Ere time shall vanish away.
I will keep my vigil beside the dead
　　Till the doom of the judgment-day."

Into the land of the dead she came,
    As the night was ebbing low,
Shrouded in dim, translucent flame,
    A flame without shape or glow.

She had forgotten sorrow or weal,
    She knew not doubting nor trust,
But the soft, gray twilight began to steal
    Over the buried dust.

As one who knoweth not woe nor good,
    She entered the mystic land ;
And lo, at each grave a spirit stood,
    A torch in his strong right hand.

" Oh why do ye stand at my graves," she said,
    " And why do ye smile at me ? "
" We are the spirits of all thy dead,
    " And have waited this day and thee."

She looked straight into their chastened eyes
    And their faces so sweet and still.
They had died as the strength of passion dies,
    In the throes of a breaking will.

An ecstacy broke over her soul,
  The rapture of perfect prayer,
And crystal morning began to roll,
  Into the listening air.

Beyond the flash of the morning star,
  Beyond the heart of the day,
Beyond the heights where the angels are,
She looked, and a Presence spake from afar
  With love that no lips may say.

A shaft of the sun smote all amain.
  O world, in the daylight, blind !
Ye seek life's glory, and seek in vain,
There are empty tombs in the dreary plain,
  And the garment, she left behind.

TIDE-RISE ON THE MAINE COAST.

ALL night I heard a voice that cried strange things ;
   At first it seemed a threat, but listening so,
   I caught a tender note, foreboding woe.
When hark ! the rush and plunge of angels' wings
   Descended into battle ! Through my pain
   I pierced, if haply, in the dusk, again,
Those mighty far-off tones would fill the sea ;
And in the breath between they came to me,
Triumphant, rhythmic, sweeping into psalm,
Till all my pulses hushed themselves to calm,
Knowing the still, small voice that he may hear
Who feels the Presence of the Lord draw near.
   I slept, if sleeping be a spirit quest ;
   I woke, if waking be a perfect rest.
And with the breaking of the day — behold !
   Only a violet deep, and facing fair
   The sunrise, one great bowlder, red and bare,
On the horizon, clear and high and cold.

MOON LIFE.

THE dome of sky, in gold enfolden,
      Grows still more golden ;
Its upper realms float, all-resplendent,
      Revealing, pendent,
The crescent censer, lifting higher,
      Day's altar fire :
Faint, faint, but yet as Time's wings darken
      And night hours hearken,
A richer, mellower glow is telling
      That light is swelling,
And rounding out a pure life-story
      In perfect glory !
God's finishing ; nor stayed nor hastened,
      Strong, perfect, chastened !
Rapt spirits, with fixed, brightening faces,
      From heavenly places
Steal down the dim mists, drawn asunder,
      In tender wonder.

Then — mystery ! there comes some token
    That God has spoken ;
The sweet glow fades ; strange shadows bound it,
    And, all around it,
Weird voices of the gloom complaining,
    Bewail its waning,
As, wistfully, the life, love-given,
    Draws into heaven.

The orient is crimson-hearted,
    Its splendors parted,
The throbbing soul of daylight springeth
    Where clear song wingeth,
And in the rose-tides, white and saintly,
    The moon gleams faintly;
A vision, 'mid the vast floods leaping, —
    Peace, hushed and sleeping.
And now great billows break, to swallow
    All heaven and follow
To overtake the day-star's warning
    With mighty morning.

INCOMPLETE.

I DO not know, but yet to me
   That seems a purpose-stricken life
   Where wish and will are ne'er at strife
And pay no price to destiny.

I do not know, but yet I deem
   That spirit poor beyond compare,
   Which never had a chain to bear,
Nor tender loss on which to dream.

I do not know — the sages teach
   The universe is open wide
   To him who cries, unsatisfied,
For something just beyond his reach.

I almost hold it in my creed
   That many a moss-encrusted name
   Lacked marble memory of fame,
Because unknown to want and need.

Oh, it may be that mirth and gold
   Purchase a heart too many friends,
   And disappointments nourish ends
A full content could never hold !

That soul which feels no restless scorn,
   Nor smiles to hide some life-long bond,
   How can he ever look beyond
To seek for what he hath been born?

A SONG AFTER WINTER.

IN MEMORY OF B. S.

WHEN thou didst take thy royal way,
   As one who heareth from a throne
The call that will not brook delay,
   And goes a sovereign to his own ;
With that triumphal going went
   Daylight and song and hope. What then
Is left for those who wait grief-spent
   And hushed among the world of men ?

Oh, should I sing from frozen tears,
   Of darkness and despair I see,
Or mourn as for unripened years,
   Dishonoring my God and thee?
Of earth grown void for one pure face,
   Of grief that knows no comforting?
Yet these are all the flesh can trace,
   And in that strange hour who might sing?

But breaking earth, and melting heaven,
    And resurrection morning, so
Have mutely taught the hope, Christ-given,
    And drawn such tenderness from woe,
That, though the sorrow winter laid
    Upon me doth not lose its chill,
A light from Paradise hath made
    Immortal thoughts rise, holy, still.

The verdure, quickening at my feet,
    Whisper the life thy spirit had ;
Its sunshine promises as sweet,
    Its high, protecting skies as glad.
And, in the loneliness of loss
    It is a solemn joy to me
To know thou hadst no racking cross,
    But art as thou wert wont to be.

No shade from long-borne anguish stole
    The glory from thy countenance,
No breath of evil dimmed thy soul,
    No baleful cloud of circumstance.

Thy mind unmarred, thy heart, whose youth
  Not yet found trust or honor frail,
Rejoicing in full love and truth!
  What has that heart to miss or fail?

Missed! Oh, to garner spring's fleet gifts
  And summer's early fruitage. Lost!
With naught to learn of autumn's rifts,
  And winter's strange, mysterious cost?
Ah, no, — fulfilled as Christ fulfils,
  Led out as His beloved one;
O God! he knows what great Love wills,
  Who learns to say, "Thy will be done!"

If Paradise to me hath been
  A rest from toil, a peace from pain,
A victory with flesh and sin,
  To-day it hath a grander gain,
Holding a purpose without blight,
  Unfettered by one weary breath,
While youth is manhood in its might,
  A might that counts not age nor death.

And this is ours, though heaven is thine ;
    A memory so full of prayer,
So linked and bound to the divine,
    That terror hath no biding there.
Thus while our doubt and fear keep strife,
    And earth grows alien in our fear,
The white bloom of thy strong, young life,
    Makes heaven home, familiar, dear.

MAY, 1888.

THE DYING OF THE FIRE.

GLIMMER, dance ; glimmer, dance ;
   Amber gold and ruby red !
Shimmer, glance ; shimmer, glance,
   Underneath and overhead.
Living shadows rise and fall
In a frolic on the wall ;
Ruby red and amber gold
Multiplied a thousand fold.
Airy pennon, shining lance,
Glimmer, dance ; glimmer, dance.
Seethe and glow, seethe and glow,
Out they go ; out they go !
Flushing dark, the old log lies,
Gleaming with a hundred eyes.
Flicker ! Flicker ! Flicker ! — Flash !
Simmer ! Simmer ! Simmer ! — Crash !
Rolls the shattered brand in twain,
Scattering a jewelled train :

Throbbing, darkening, pulsing, burning,
As with changing passions yearning,
Throbbing, darkening, pulsing, dying.
  See between the feeble flashes,
Sparks, like spirits, heavenward flying,
  Leave their tenements in ashes.
One by one they flick and flare,
Fading out of sight and air,
While above the dreary hosts
Flit a troop of pallid ghosts.
Cold and gray they rise and quiver,
  Exhalations of the tomb,
Restlessly they soar and shiver,
  Drifting back to sullen gloom.
            But, aloft,
              A single spark,
          Rosy, soft,
              Seeks the dark,
          And to higher
              Regions fled,
          Leaves the fire
              Dark,
                  Dead !

LOVE'S COST.

So much we miss
If love is weak, so much we gain
If love is strong, God thinks no pain
Too sharp or lasting to ordain
To teach us this.

H. H.

On the edge of the desert he paused, and turned,
    There were palms, long shadows, and running water,
    And the arms of his love, the great sheik's daughter;
Here, blasting sands to the red sky burned.
A faltered word, and he could not go,
A tear, a smile, and her lips would stay;
But they locked from speech, though their sad eyes
        yearned,
Forbidden comfort, nor gave their woe
        One moment of sweet delay.

Through the luminous dark of that hemisphere
    More mute than time to the starved desire,
    A rider moaneth from heart of fire:
" Soul of my life, was it love or fear?

12

Was it fate, or thy spirit stronger than fate
That held my longing and hushed thy cry?
Oh, hold the tempest that it may hear,
Oh, bid the pulse of the lightning wait,
But if love must tarry, I die!"

In a captive city the victor stands,
   For Allah's sake and a name unspoken,
   The siege and famine and plague are broken,
He scatters bread with a warrior's hands.
" In the faith a crusader taught to me
When I lay at his mercy, Arise! be glad!
Eat and rejoice by yon sacred token!
O Christ, these babes I have saved to Thee,
For the children I never had!"

Those are wild, deep words that the ages borrow,
   From an old-world groping and pathos wrung;
   "The night and the desert are never young,
But love and the stars will be born with the morrow."
One from the battlefield, one from the tomb,
Two mighty spirits their pinions toss
In a rapture strong as the death of sorrow;
And, lo, on crown and aramanth flower
The glory-flame of the cross!

UNDER THE CRATER.

LOVE and glory, delight and song
   Are the sea and sky, with a band between
Where a broken girdle of coast dips long
   And low, in azure and shimmering green.
Chafed with a foam of silver snow,
   The violet shadows of tacking sails
   Melt in a blush, where the daylight trails
Its warmth and beauty ; so loath to go !
   And a soft, wet wind from the Indian South,
   Stirs the vapor over the crater's mouth.

Dream-peace, dream-color around me !   Strange !
   So near are the throes of a demon's birth,
A demon to sport with that mighty range,
   And tear the heart of the happy earth,
With a splendor of rushing, poisoned fires,
   Serpentine blue, quick, mortal red,

Basilisk green, and clear gold, wed
To an after-cloud of opaline spires ;
    Where life goes out with a strangled moan,
    And the death of the centuries seethes alone.

Who shall fathom the south wind's will, —
    To leave the unharbored boats asleep,
But to lift and waver that shade, until
    It drops for awhile on the awful steep?
Ah, compassionate breath of Heaven, that flies
    Tender and sweet with orange flowers,
    Hushing the terrible lava showers,
Baring the stars in far cool skies !
    What woe or remorse may despair of rest,
    When God smiles over the crater's breast?

WAITING FOR SUNRISE.

NAKED, and dim, and chill,
  Night flings her sifted spray ;
But in the ploughed field, life is born,
  Life out of darkness wrung.
A bough against my sill
  Pulses with wakening May.
In tree and thicket, twig and thorn,
  Faith waits the rising sun.

Translucent waters thrill
  Up from the sleeping bay.
Our sails have caught the summer morn
  But even now begun.
Clear lights the sea-curves fill,
  Clear sounds in echoes play,
Winding her golden-throated horn
  Hope waits the rising sun.

Over a shrunken rill
　　The sky dips, low and gray.
Gray are the uplands, and forlorn,
　　The distance gray and dun.
Soft russet crowns the hill,
　　A stain of after-day ;
Amid her garnered fruit and corn,
　　Love waits the rising sun.

White, underfoot, and still,
　　White where the branches sway
Their cobweb drapings lightly worn,
　　And mantles, winter-spun.
Moonbeams with loving will
　　On lily meadows stray,
Of every blemished garment shorn,
　　Peace waits the rising sun.

L'ENVOI.

O night, whose voices shrill
　　Sweep down our lonely way,
We laugh thy terrors all to scorn,
　　We wait the rising sun !